I LIKE TO BE LITTLE

Charlotte Zolotow

I LIKE TO BE LITTLE

Illustrated by
Erik Blegvad

THOMAS Y. CROWELL   NEW YORK

A version of *I Like To Be Little* was previously published
by Abelard-Schuman in 1966 with the title *I Want To Be Little*.

I Like To Be Little

Library of Congress Cataloging-in-Publication Data
Zolotow, Charlotte, 1915–
    I like to be little.

    Summary: A little girl, answering her mother's
question about why she likes to be little, describes
some of the special pleasures of being a child.
    [1. Growth—Fiction]   I. Blegvad, Erik, ill.
II. Title.
PZ7.Z77Iak 1987   [E]   83-45056
ISBN 0-690-04672-3
ISBN 0-690-04674-X (lib. bdg.)

For Dee's granddaughters
Kasey and Becky

Once there was a little girl.

"What do you want to be when you grow up?" her mother asked.

"I just want to stay little right now," she said.

"Why?" said her mother. "It's nice to be grown up. Why do you want to be little?"

"Because I am," said the little girl, "and because when you are little you can do things you can't when you grow up."

"What can you do that grown-ups don't?" said her mother.

"Skip," said the little girl. "I can skip when I'm glad. Grown-ups don't skip when they're glad."

"That's so," said her mother, "though they have different ways to be glad."

"Oh," said the little girl. "I like to skip. That's why I like to be little."

"What else though?" said her mother.

"I can sit under the dining-room table and make it my house and draw my finger around the roses in the rug. Grown-ups can't sit under the table."

"True," said the mother, "but grown-ups don't want to."

"I want to," said the little girl, "that's why I like being little."

"What else?" said her mother.

"I can go barefoot in summertime. Grown-ups don't go barefoot in the summer."

"True," said the mother. "They usually don't."

"I like to go barefoot," said the little girl. "I like to be little."

"What else though?" said the mother.

"The ice-cream man knows my first name," said the little girl. "He doesn't know yours."

"No," said the mother.

"I like him to know," the little girl said. "I like to be little."

"What else?" asked her mother.

"I can sit and do nothing," said the little girl. "Grown-ups never sit and do nothing."

"They're too busy," said her mother.

"I like to sit and do nothing," said the little girl. "I like to be little."

"What else though?" asked her mother.

"If I see something pretty I can draw it with crayons. Grown-ups don't draw with crayons," said the little girl.

"Usually not," said her mother.

"I like to draw with crayons," said the little girl. "That's why I like to be little."

"What else?" said her mother.

"Grown-ups don't have birthday parties with cake and ice cream and candles," said the little girl.

"No," said the mother, "they don't really want them."

"I want them," said the little girl, "that's why I like to be little."

"What else?" asked her mother.

"I can sit at the window and watch the rain run down the pane," said the little girl. "I never saw a grown-up do that."

"Is that fun?" asked the mother.

"For me," said the little girl happily. "That's why I like to be little."

"What else then?" asked her mother.

"I can dress up in funny costumes on Halloween," said the little girl, "and go trick-or-treating. Grown-ups don't."

"True," said her mother, smiling.

"I like to dress up in funny costumes and go trick-or-treating," said the little girl. "I like to be little."

"What else?" said the mother.

"I can jump in the piles of leaves each fall," the little girl said. "Grown-ups just rake them."

"Rake them into piles," said her mother.

"I like to jump in the leaves," the little girl said. "I like to be little."

"What else?" said her mother.

"I can eat the snow when it first falls,"
said the little girl. "Grown-ups never do
that."

"Is it good?" her mother asked.

"It is," said the little girl. "I like being
little very much. I like the things that
happen."

"Well," said her mother, "I know
something about being grown-up that
makes all those things happen again."

"What?" said the little girl. "What could
that be?"

Her mother put her hand under the
little girl's chin and looked in her eyes.

"When you're grown up," she said, "you can be the mother of a little girl like you."

The little girl smiled.

"Well," said the little girl, "I know something as good as that."

"What?" said her mother. "What could be as good as having a little girl like you?"

"Well," said the little girl, "at night, after you kiss me and tuck me in, I can lie in bed and think of growing up to be like you.

When you're little you know you'll grow up.
Grown-ups already *are*. I like to know
I'll grow up someday. But right now I like
being little."